Chickadees At Night

by Bill O. Smith

illustrated by Charles R. Murphy

For all who sing in tough times
B. O. S. and C. R. M.

Text and Illustration Copyright © 2012 by Bill O. Smith
Book Design by Draw Big Design
All rights reserved, including the right of reproduction in whole
or in part in any form.

7th Printing
Published by Sleepytime Press
E-mail: sleepytimepress@gmail.com
Web site: www.sleepytimepress.com

ISBN 978-0-615-56972-7
Library of Congress Control Number: 2012901871

The sun comes up.
Chickadees tweet.
Chickadees flit.
Chickadees eat.

They dip and dart
through a tangle of trees,

chittery flittery chickadees.

But sometime near the end of day,
chickadees fly away, away —
through the branches, out of sight ...

… where do chickadees go at night?

After dipping and darting
and dining for hours,
do they climb to the clouds?
Do they scrub in the showers?

tweeeeeze...

Or, filing into hollow birches,
do they come to rest on hidden perches?
Not a peep heard anymore,
except for the tweeeeeze of Grandfather's snore.

Do they rise as one on the call of the loon
till they come to rest on a crescent moon?

And that moon, with its smiling sideways lips,
is that really a … chickadee-clipse?

No! That can't be! That's too far for a chickadee. After they fly away, away, I'll bet they say:

LET'S PLAY!

Let's tickle our tummies in windy trees-swinging, swaying, in the breeze.

Let's turn each spider web unseen

into a chickadee trampoline!

Look!

A tip of tail!
A point of beak!

Are chickadees playing
hide-and-seek? ......

And what is more fun than a moonlit whirl
on the furry back of a flying squirrel?

Unless it's even funner yet, to glide on an owl like a jumbo jet.

On summer nights, do grown-ups munch
on gourmet grubs and beetle crunch?
Now everyone knows that chickadees chirp.
But after those snacks do chickadees …

……?

And out of the sight of Mom and Pop,
do teens boogaloo at the chickadee hop?

Do the girls fluff up and shake their stuff
while the boys hang out and try to look tough?

When chickadee chicks are feeling blah,
do they clip their claws at the chickadee spa?

When a chickadee child is feeling down,
do lullabies rise over chickadee town?

When summer green turns into gold,
do great and small and young and old ...

... gather for ancient tales retold of chickadees kind
and chickadees bold?

Green to gold, gold to white,
how *do* they keep warm on a winter night?

With chickadee caps on chickadee heads,
do they sleep eight across on chickadee beds?

From northern woods to the Alabamas,

what do chickadees wear for pajamas?

When so many millions fly away,
why do these tough little chickadees stay?

Are they out there now, on this starry night,
just past the spill of bedroom light?

Close your eyes.
Snuggle in.

Can you see
on a little branch
in a nearby tree
one bold
one kind
little chickadee?

No matter what this long night brings,
are we safe beneath its sheltering wings?

I hear the answer inside of me ...

fee-bee... fee-bee... chicka-dee-dee-dee...

Can you hear it too, inside of you? ...

fee-bee... fee-bee...

...shhhhhhhhh...

...chicka-dee-dee-dee......

We hear, little bird, your ancient song —
wherever you are, is where you belong.

Chickadee Nuggets

A chickadee will fit into a child's hands. It weighs about as much as a quarter.

Chickadees live in every state in the continental United States, and in every province of Canada.

There are seven species of chickadees. The most common is the black-capped chickadee (Poecile atricapillus).

Chickadees stay put. They are popular visitors at millions of bird feeders twelve months a year.

Although chickadees love sunflower seeds at feeders, their favorite food is insects.

Chickadees usually roost high in evergreen trees, low in spruce trees, or in small tree cavities, often birch.

During nesting season, males serenade females with a dawn chorus that can last from twenty minutes to an hour.

Chickadee pairs usually make nests in holes in soft or rotting wood, usually 3 to 10 feet off the ground. Father chickadee often feeds Mother while she is sitting on eggs.

Chickadee pairs remain with one flock permanently. The young move to other flocks.

In the fall, the "memory" part of a chickadee's brain gets much bigger. Chickadees can remember for twenty-eight days or more where they store food.

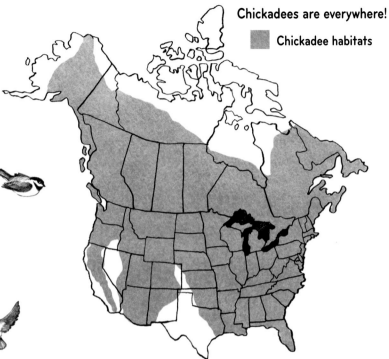

Chickadees are everywhere!

Chickadee habitats

In winter, chickadees will gain an additional 10% of body weight each day by stuffing themselves, and then keep warm at night by shivering the fat away.

A lovely fee-bee and a buzzy chicka-dee-dee-dee are the best known chickadee songs. But chickadees actually use at least fifteen calls to talk to each other about such concerns as danger, territory, and food supply.

A patient child might get a chickadee to eat out of his or her hands.

A patient child might also find more than ten chickadees, but fewer than twenty, on the hide-and-seek page of this book.